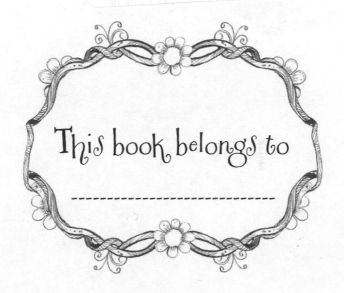

This book belongs to

- -

Bluebell Glade

Dandelion Dell

Heart of Misty Wood

Hawthorn Hedgerows

Heather Hill

Sundown Hill

Crystal Cave

Golden Meadow

Moonshine Pond

Dewdrop Spring

Honeydew Meadow

Mulberry Bushes

Misty Wood Rabbit Warren

HOME SWEET HOME

How many *Fairy Animals* books have you collected?

- Chloe the Kitten
- Bella the Bunny
- Paddy the Puppy
- Mia the Mouse
- Hailey the Hedgehog
- Sophie the Squirrel
- ✓ Poppy the Pony
- Daisy the Deer
- Betsy the Bunny
- Katie the Kitten

Look out for more magical adventures coming soon!

Fairy Animals
of Misty Wood

Poppy the Pony

Lily Small

EGMONT

With special thanks to Thea Bennett

EGMONT
We bring stories to life

Poppy the Pony first published in Great Britain 2014
by Egmont UK Limited
The Yellow Building, 1 Nicholas Road, London W11 4AN

Text copyright © 2014 Hothouse Fiction Ltd
Illustrations copyright © 2014 Kirsteen Harris Jones
All rights reserved

ISBN 978 1 4052 6817 2
1 3 5 7 9 10 8 6 4 2

www.egmont.co.uk

www.hothousefiction.com

www.fairyanimals.com

A CIP catalogue record for this title is available from the British Library

Printed and bound in Great Britain by The CPI Group

55712/4

MIX
Paper
FSC FSC® C018306

EGMONT LUCKY COIN

Our story began over a century ago, when seventeen-year-old
Egmont Harald Petersen found a coin in the street.

He was on his way to buy a flyswatter, a small hand-operated
printing machine that he then set up in his tiny apartment.

The coin brought him such good luck that today Egmont has
offices in over 30 countries around the world. And that lucky
coin is still kept at the company's head offices in Denmark.

Contents

CHAPTER ONE

Poppy Needs a Friend

It was a lovely bright morning in Misty Wood. On top of Sundown Hill, a little pony called Poppy was grazing beside her mum.

POPPY THE PONY

Sundown Hill was the sunniest place in the whole wood. The yellow primroses that grew there shone like sunbeams, and there was plenty of lush green grass, too. Poppy liked the grass very much.

'Yum, yum!' she whinnied as she nibbled the juicy stems. She was nearly full now, but the grass was so tasty she couldn't stop eating.

'That's right, Poppy!' neighed her mum. 'We've got lots of work to do today, so you need a big breakfast.'

Poppy was a Petal Pony – one of the fairy animals of Misty Wood. Her gleaming coat was the same pale yellow as the primroses and her silky mane and tail were as white as swan feathers. It was the Petal Ponies' special job to swish their glossy tails and waft the beautiful scent of the flowers through the wood. The sweet smells made all the other animals feel happy.

'*Woof, woof*!' Loud barking rang out across the hill.

Poppy stopped chewing and turned to see who it was.

'Let's have a race!' a voice called. 'I bet I win. *Woof*!'

Poppy heard the patter of paws on the ground. Lots of paws! Her long legs started to tremble as a pack of Pollen Puppies came scampering through the grass.

'*Woof*!' they barked as they charged along with their tails wagging. 'Hello, Petal Pony. *Woof, woof*!'

But instead of saying hello back, all Poppy could think was, *Help!*

You see, Poppy was a very shy pony and she found it hard to talk to fairy animals she didn't know. Quick as a flash, she unfurled her

sky-blue wings and flew behind
her mum to hide.

'Hey, Petal Pony!' barked one
of the puppies. 'Where did you go?'
He peeped through the silky fronds
of Poppy's mum's long tail. When
he saw Poppy hiding, he trotted
round to speak to her.

'There you are,' he said with
a grin. 'We're having a race to
Honeydew Meadow. Would you
like to come with us?'

POPPY THE PONY

Poppy shook her head.

'Why don't you, Poppy?' said her mum. 'You're really good at galloping.'

'Yes, you could win the race,' barked the puppy. 'Come on!'

Poppy hid her face in her long white mane. She felt so shy, she didn't know what to do.

Poppy's mum looked at her kindly. 'It'll be fun,' she said.

Poppy thought for a moment.

Her legs were a lot longer than a puppy's. And she did love to gallop fast . . .

'Poppy?' Her mum gave her a nudge with her velvety nose. 'What do you say?'

Poppy took a deep breath. She wanted to say, 'Yes, please. I'd love to!' But her throat went tight and all that came out was a little snuffling noise that sounded like: '*Hm-hm-hm.*'

The puppy wagged his tail. 'What did you say? Are you coming?'

Poppy hung her head. She was so embarrassed she felt hot all over.

Poppy's mum looked at her, waiting for her to say something, but Poppy's voice had completely disappeared.

'Maybe not today,' Poppy's mum told the puppy. 'But thank

11

you very much for asking.'

'That's OK! Poppy can play anytime.' The puppy waved a paw at Poppy to say goodbye. 'Come on, puppies, let's go!'

The puppies scampered away
over the hill, barking happily.

'I wish I could have gone
with them,' Poppy sighed. 'But
I'm so shy I can't even speak
to anybody.'

Her mum nuzzled her neck.
'You have to try to be a bit braver,
Poppy. How will the other animals
know that you want to be friends if
you don't talk to them?' She lifted
her head and gazed down the hill

at the rest of Misty Wood. 'Never mind now – it's time to start work,' she said. 'The sun's shining and all the flowers are out.'

Poppy's face brightened. She loved swishing the lovely flower smells around the wood.

Her mum looked thoughtful for a second. 'Why don't we split up and go to different places today?' she said. 'I'll go to Bluebell Glade. You could start at Heather

Hill. There'll be lots of gorgeous heather blossoms there.'

'I'd rather be with you,' Poppy said, her tail drooping. She'd never gone without her mum before.

'You'll be fine,' her mum told her gently. 'And maybe other fairy animals will come and talk to you. You might make a friend.'

'Maybe,' said Poppy, but she didn't think so. How could she make a friend if all she managed to say was, *hm-hm-hm*?

'Just give it a try!' her mum said. 'Have a lovely day and I'll see you at teatime.' She nuzzled Poppy with her nose and then galloped off a little way, before opening her wings and soaring into the sky.

Poppy felt a bit lonely, left behind on Sundown Hill. But the sun was shining and she had lots of work to do, so she shook out her

16

white mane, fluttered her wings and headed off.

Misty Wood looked beautiful as she flew over it. When she arrived at Heather Hill, she heard a loud buzzing. Hundreds of bumblebees were hovering over the purple heather flowers.

Poppy landed in a quiet spot at the side of the hill and began flicking her snowy white tail over the flowers. A wonderful sweet smell like honey filled the air.

'*Mmmmm*!' droned the bumblebees. They flew up and began swirling in a huge cloud. Then they zoomed down to collect pollen, buzzing even more loudly.

Poppy smiled as she listened. The bees sounded really happy and it was all because of her!

It was time to move on and find some more flowers.

Poppy cantered down Heather

POPPY NEEDS A FRIEND

Hill and into the trees. They formed a beautiful green archway for her to run through. Thin fingers of sunlight beamed through the leaves above her, making a pretty golden pattern on the floor.

Poppy felt very content as she raced along. But then, just as she reached a clearing, she saw three large fairy animals with stripy faces and silver wings.

Bark Badgers! Poppy skidded

to a halt. They mustn't see her, or they might want to come over and talk. Luckily, she spotted a big honeysuckle bush that she could hide behind. She trotted over to it as quietly as she could.

Poppy peeped through the leaves. The badgers were busy doing their special job, decorating the tree bark.

Poppy watched as one badger scraped his claws over the bark,

21

making a flowing line that looked
just like a pony's tail. Another was
scratching swirly shapes that made
Poppy think of a rushing stream.
The smallest badger was making
a circle with lots of marks inside.

When he'd finished, it looked as
if a face was smiling out from the
tree trunk.

That's so clever! thought Poppy.
She noticed that the honeysuckle
bush she was hiding behind was

covered in white flowers with long yellow stems. She sniffed. The flowers smelled so lovely – even sweeter than the heather blossoms. Careful not to make a sound, she slowly swung her tail back and forth and the scent began to drift towards the badgers. The smallest one looked around.

'Mmmm,' he murmured, 'something smells nice!'

Poppy kept very still and after

a minute the badger turned back to his tree trunk and began to draw a new pattern with his claws.

'Phew!' Poppy breathed a sigh of relief. He hadn't seen her.

The badgers smiled as they sniffed the honeysuckle perfume. One by one, they began carving beautiful pictures of flowers on their trees. They looked so happy. Poppy's work was done.

She started creeping away

from the clearing . . . but the smallest badger looked around again. And this time he spotted her!

'Hello,' he called, twirling his silver whiskers in greeting.

Poppy wanted to hide, but she was so shy she couldn't move.

The badger smiled. 'You're a Petal Pony.'

Poppy nodded. She tried to say something, but nothing came out. It was as if all the words inside her

26

had run away.

'Thank you for making everything smell so good,' the badger said.

Poppy swallowed. She *had* to say something!

'You're welcome,' she whispered very quietly.

The badger waited, but Poppy couldn't say anything else.

'Well – thanks again,' he said with a friendly wave of his paw, and he turned back to his friends.

Poppy's head fell. The three badgers were having so much fun, chatting and laughing as they made their beautiful patterns. If only she could go and join in.

'I'll never, ever be able to make a friend,' she whispered to herself. A silvery tear ran down her primrose cheek and dripped off the end of her velvety nose.

CHAPTER TWO

The Bluebirds' Song

Poppy shook the tears from her
eyes and began to trot through
the bright green ferns that grew in
clusters beneath the trees.

She couldn't keep feeling sad – she had to find some more flowers. Suddenly she spotted something ahead. It looked like a huge mirror, shining brightly on the ground.

'Moonshine Pond!' Poppy neighed. 'And it's daytime, so the Moonbeam Moles will all be fast asleep. At least I won't have to worry about bumping into any of them.'

31

The Moonbeam Moles lived
in burrows on the banks of the
pond. Their special job was to
catch moonbeams and place
them in the water to make it glow
like a beautiful pearl. Of course,
the moles could only collect
moonbeams after dark, so they
woke up at night and went to bed
during the day. Right now they
would all be tucked up, fast asleep
in their burrows.

Poppy cantered up to the pond. It was very quiet there. The only thing that moved was Poppy's reflection. Her yellow coat and long white mane looked pretty in the gleaming water.

Not far from the pond, Poppy could see little heaps of earth that marked the entrances to the moles' burrows. She went over and bent her head to see if she could hear the moles inside.

A funny grunting and whistling noise was coming up from under the ground.

'*Och, och, phweee . . .*'

'*Phwee, och, och . . .*'

The moles were snoring!

They certainly wouldn't disturb her while she did her work.

Poppy saw some lavender bushes close by. She trotted over and swung her long tail to and fro over the lilac flowers.

'*Aaaah!*' she heard the moles sigh. '*Mmmmm!*' they breathed, as the soothing lavender scent reached their sleepy noses, deep underground.

Poppy smiled. Her work at

Moonshine Pond was finished. She flicked her wings and soared up through the trees, heading for the Heart of Misty Wood.

Soon she came to a place where the trees grew very tall. Beneath the trees was a grassy glade and Poppy drifted towards it. As she landed, the grass felt as soft as a cushion under her hoofs.

High above in the treetops, Poppy heard the flutter of wings.

36

She looked up. Two bluebirds had landed on a branch.

'*Tweet-tweet*,' sang one, flicking his bright blue tail.

'*Cheep-cheep*,' replied the other, nodding her little blue head.

Poppy pricked her ears to

listen to their lovely song. But they were so high up it sounded very faint. If only they would come closer.

Then Poppy had an idea. She walked over to a rose bush that was growing at the edge of the glade. She brushed her tail over the velvety pink petals, and a beautiful scent rolled like mist across the glade.

One of the bluebirds looked down, his head tilted to the side.

Poppy swept her tail over the roses again.

'*Twee-ee-eet!*' sang the bluebird as the perfume drifted up to him. He leaped off the branch and flew down to the grass.

'*Chee-ee-eep!*' trilled his mate as she joined him.

The two birds hopped around and fluttered their blue wings as if they were dancing. They hadn't noticed Poppy.

39

They like the smell of roses,
Poppy thought with a smile.

There was a rustle at the edge
of the glade and a shiny brown
nose peeped through a cluster of
ferns. A Stardust Squirrel with
wings as bright as starshine
emerged. Poppy darted behind
some trees so he wouldn't see her.
But then a voice spoke up on the
other side of the nearest tree trunk.

'Ho hum, tiddly-pum! Just

look at all these leaves . . .'

Poppy peeped round the tree trunk. A Hedgerow Hedgehog was rolling around on the ground, collecting dead leaves on her spines.

'*Tweet, tweet! Cheep, cheeep!*' warbled the bluebirds.

'What a lovely song!' the hedgehog sighed. 'I think I'll take a break.' She sat down to listen. She still had leaves stuck all over her back like a coat.

41

Who's going to turn up next?
thought Poppy. She made herself
as small as she could so the
hedgehog wouldn't notice her.

'*Tweety-tweet-cheep!*' trilled the
bluebirds.

Now Poppy could hear rustling
noises all around her. She felt her
heart beating fast. There were
fairy animals everywhere, making
their way into the glade. A herd of
Dream Deer trotted past, lifting

their graceful heads as they sniffed the roses. Some Bark Badgers pushed their stripy faces through the ferns to watch the birds. Pollen Puppies, tails wagging, flopped on the ground to listen.

More and more animals arrived. Cobweb Kittens floated down through the air. Moss Mice and Holly Hamsters fluttered out from behind the trees, their tiny wings twinkling.

'*Tweeety-tweet! Cheepy-cheep!*'
sang the bluebirds.

'Ah, what a wonderful song,'
a Bark Badger murmured. 'And it
smells so *lovely* here.'

'Shhh,' squeaked a little Moss
Mouse, swinging from a grass
stem. 'Just listen!'

All the animals fell silent.
As they listened to the bluebirds,
Poppy saw her chance. She flicked
her wings and flew away from the

46

glade. Thank goodness no one had noticed her!

Poppy flew swiftly through the wood. She was just beginning to feel tired when she saw a gnarled old tree with juicy golden pears hanging from its branches. It had been a long time since breakfast and she was feeling very hungry, so she swooped down and landed under the tree.

She was just about to take a

bite from one of the fallen pears

when she heard a voice from

above.

'Help!' the voice squeaked.

Poppy froze. Someone was up

the tree and they were calling to

her! But what was she going to do?

CHAPTER THREE

Poppy to the Rescue!

Everything went quiet. Poppy
was just wondering whether she'd
imagined the voice when she heard
it again.

'Help!' it cried. 'Please help me!'

Poppy was puzzled. She hadn't seen anyone at all when she flew over the pear tree.

'Who are you?' she tried to say, but her voice wasn't working again and all that came out was, '*Hm-hm-hm?*'

'I'm stuck!' the voice whimpered. 'Please help me.'

Whoever it was sounded very scared.

Poppy peered up. A tiny
Cobweb Kitten, with fur the colour
of chocolate, was clinging to a
high branch.

51

'Please! I want to get down,' the kitten meowed, letting go of the branch and waving her paws at Poppy.

Poppy was amazed. The kitten wasn't holding on – so why hadn't she fallen out of the tree? Then Poppy saw that one of the kitten's golden wings was trapped.

Poppy felt so sorry for the kitten that she forgot all about being shy. 'You poor thing,' she neighed. 'Of course I'll help you.'

'Oh, thank you!' gasped the
kitten.

'What's your name? And how
did you get stuck up there?' Poppy
called. Her voice was working
perfectly now – she didn't even
have to think about it.

The kitten was trembling.
'My name's Coco,' she meowed.
'What's yours?'

'Poppy,' Poppy replied.

'Hello, Poppy. I was just on my way to meet my friends for a picnic when I spotted these juicy pears.'

Poppy nodded. 'They do look delicious.'

'I thought they'd be perfect for the picnic,' Coco said. 'I flew down to pick one, but then my wing got caught.'

Poppy tossed her white mane. Then, with a swirl of her

54

shimmering wings, she swooped up to the branch. But as soon as she landed, Poppy realised she couldn't reach Coco with her nose. There were too many twigs and leaves in the way.

'Please be quick!' Coco pleaded. 'My wing is getting sore.'

Carefully, Poppy turned and twirled her tail over Coco's wing, twisting it gently until it came free.

Coco leaped off the branch . . .

then squealed with fright.

Poppy saw Coco tumbling down! She flapped her wings hard and flew after her. When she was close enough, she flicked out her tail as far as it would go and managed to catch Coco just before she hit the ground.

'Thank you so much!' Coco gasped as Poppy lowered her onto the grass. 'My wing isn't working properly. I can't fly.'

POPPY TO THE RESCUE!

A tear welled in Coco's eye. 'And if I can't fly, I'll never get to the picnic in time.'

The little kitten looked so sad that Poppy didn't stop to think. 'I could take you there if you like,' she said in a very soft voice.

Coco was so pleased she jumped up and down. 'Ouch!' she squeaked as she tried to flutter her wings. 'I must remember not to do that. Thank you, Poppy!'

'You're welcome,' Poppy said.

Coco was being so bouncy
it made Poppy feel shy again, so
she didn't say anything else. She
wrapped her tail round the kitten
and lifted her onto her back.

'Ooh, this is so much fun!'
Coco meowed, holding on to
Poppy's coat with her paws. 'I've
always wondered what it must be
like to be a Petal Pony – to gallop
so fast and fly so high. Now I'm

going to find out!'

Poppy tossed her head. She couldn't help feeling a little bit proud that Coco might want to be like her. 'Let's go!' she neighed.

Coco told Poppy that the picnic was happening by Dewdrop Spring. Poppy set off through the trees at a smooth trot. Soon they came out into Honeydew Meadow.

'Could we go a bit faster?' asked Coco.

'Are you sure?' Poppy said.

'I don't want you to fall off.'

'I'll hold on tight, I promise,'

Coco said.

Poppy stretched out her neck

and began to race across the
golden flowers.

'Wheeee!' Coco squealed as
Poppy leaped over a fallen log.
'Woo-hooo!' she whooped as
Poppy kicked up her heels and
jumped over a hedge.

Poppy's hoofs thundered
across the golden meadow. When
she couldn't gallop any faster, she
unfurled her wings and soared into
the air.

'Oooooh!' Coco meowed.

Poppy felt the little kitten clinging to her mane as they floated high over a hill where lots of green bushes grew.

'Those are the Mulberry Bushes,' Poppy said. 'That's where the Misty Wood rabbit warren is.'

'We're nearly there then!' squeaked Coco. 'Dewdrop Spring runs right by the rabbit warren. Look, there are my friends!'

Poppy glanced down. She could see the silvery thread of Dewdrop Spring winding its way past the warren. Then she saw three fairy animals spreading out a picnic blanket made of moss on the banks of the spring. There was Bud Bunny, a Moss Mouse and a Holly Hamster.

Poppy's wings began to tremble. It was OK being with Coco. It was easy talking to just one little kitten. But what would happen if she had to meet three new fairy animals all in one go?

CHAPTER FOUR

Picnic Time!

Poppy's heart pounded as she

glided towards Dewdrop Spring.

'Hey – look at meeee!' Coco

called to her friends down below.

The three fairy animals

were very surprised indeed when they looked up and saw Coco on Poppy's back.

'How did you get to ride on a Petal Pony?' squeaked the Moss Mouse.

'That looks like fun!' chuckled the Bud Bunny.

'Come down and start the picnic! I'm starving!' shouted the Holly Hamster, rubbing his furry tummy.

Poppy's blue wings glimmered as she circled in the air, looking for somewhere to land. She felt very shy with all of Coco's friends watching her.

Next to the picnic spot there was a grassy bank covered with bright yellow buttercups. Poppy fluttered down towards it.

'I'll drop you here, Coco,' she whinnied. As soon as her hoofs touched the ground, she carefully

lifted Coco down with her tail.
'I've got to go now,' she explained
hurriedly. 'I've got loads of work to
do and –'

But it was too late.

The Bud Bunny came
hopping towards them through
the buttercups. 'Coco – who's your
friend?' she asked.

Poppy hid her face in her
mane. If only she'd flown away
more quickly!

Then the Moss Mouse scampered up, his long whiskers twitching. 'Are you all right, Coco?'

'I got stuck in a tree!' Coco explained. 'I was trying to pick some pears for our picnic, but my wing got caught. It was horrible.' Coco's tail fluffed up like a feather duster at the thought.

'That sounds awful. Oh, look, here comes hungry Harry!' said the bunny, as the Holly Hamster trotted up on his chubby little legs.

'Who said pears? Did you say
pears?' he said to Coco, puffing
out his cheeks. 'I love pears. Did
you bring some?'

Coco shook her head. 'No, I was too scared to pick any. I thought I'd be stuck up there forever.'

'How did you escape?' asked the mouse.

'Poppy rescued me,' Coco purred. 'She's amazing!' The kitten twined herself round Poppy's legs, rubbing them with her soft fur, as she told her friends how the pony had freed her from the tree.

Coco's friends all looked at Poppy in admiration.

'I'm Max,' squeaked the Moss Mouse, standing as tall as he could on his back legs and twirling his whiskers at Poppy.

'I'm Bobbi,' said the Bud Bunny, twitching her velvety pink nose.

'And I'm hungry – *starving* hungry!' said Harry.

Poppy looked down at the

buttercups and tried to pretend that she wasn't really there. Her heart was beating so fast and she felt too hot. If only they would all stop staring at her!

Harry looked over longingly at the picnic blanket. 'Let's eat before my tummy gets so empty it starts to cry!' he groaned.

They all turned to the picnic. Poppy was relieved. Finally, she had a chance to escape. She spread her wings, ready to take off. But just then, Max looked back.

'Don't go!' he cried when he saw her.

Poppy opened her mouth and tried to speak, but all that came out was, '*Hm-hm-hm!*'

Coco padded over and rubbed against Poppy's legs again. 'You must come to our picnic,' she purred.

'Please stay, Poppy!' Bobbi said.

'If you don't all hurry up, I am going to faint from starvation!' Harry called, sucking his cheeks in as thin as they would go – which wasn't very thin at all.

It was no good. Poppy's voice had disappeared again, and she didn't want to seem rude. All she could do was fold her wings back down and trot after the others to

78

the picnic spot.

The mossy blanket was laden with conker-shell bowls full of nuts and seeds, bunches of tasty carrots with leafy green tops, and a basket of beautiful rosy apples.

Coco, Bobbi, Max and Harry settled down and started tucking in. But Poppy felt much too shy to sit down with them. So she stood behind, shifting nervously from hoof to hoof. She was very glad that they were all too busy enjoying the food to notice her.

If I went back to the buttercup patch, she thought, *I could wave my tail over the flowers to spread the perfume. Everyone would be happy and they'd forget all about me.*

She was just about to slip away when Coco looked round. 'Would you like an apple?' she asked.

Before Poppy could even try

to answer, the little kitten came

padding over with a shiny red

apple in her mouth. She put it

down in front of Poppy.

Poppy licked the apple, but she didn't bite into it. If she made a loud crunching noise, everyone would look at her again.

'Oooh!' squealed Coco suddenly. 'What was that?' She wiped at her head with her paw.

Poppy felt a fat drop of water plop onto her mane.

Everyone looked up. The sun had disappeared and a big black cloud was filling up the sky. It was starting to rain!

'Oh, no!' squeaked Max, holding a carrot over his head as the drops began falling thick and fast. 'Our picnic will be ruined!'

CHAPTER FIVE

Under the Oak Tree

'I'm getting wet,' meowed Coco, shaking raindrops out of her fur.

'Me too,' squeaked Max. 'We'd better get out of here.'

'Never mind about you getting wet – what about the food?' Harry cried. He started scampering about, gathering all the food in the middle of the mossy blanket. Then he folded the corners together and tied them tightly in a knot.

'Where can we go?' asked Bobbi, flicking the rain from her floppy ears. 'There's nowhere here to shelter.'

85

The rain was coming down really hard now. *At least it will make the flowers grow*, Poppy thought. But she felt very sorry for the four friends. Their picnic was spoiled and now they were going to get soaked. If she was brave enough, maybe she could help . . .

She took a deep breath. 'Jump on my back!' she whinnied. As soon as the words burst from her mouth, she felt so shy she had to

86

look down at her hoofs.

'Really, Poppy?' said Bobbi, her eyes shining.

'Come on, quick!' said Coco, scampering up Poppy's tail and on to her back.

Bobbi did a giant hop and landed just behind Coco.

Harry and Max fluttered their little wings and floated up to join the others. 'Don't forget the food!' Harry shrieked.

'I won't,' Poppy said. 'Hold
on tight!' She picked up the
blanket bundle with her mouth,
and started cantering away from
Dewdrop Spring.

'Wheeee!' squealed Coco.

'Isn't this fun?'

'Bouncing bunnies!' cried
Bobbi. 'It's brilliant!'

Poppy's tail streamed behind
her as she galloped towards the
trees. She knew just where to go.

Right in the heart of the wood grew a tall oak tree with wide leafy branches big enough to cover them all.

As soon as she spotted the tree, she slowed down to a gentle trot.

'This is perfect! We'll be dry here,' squeaked Max as Poppy came to halt.

Poppy carefully placed the blanket of food on the ground under the tree. Max and Harry fluttered down, and Bobbi and Coco both reached the ground in one big leap.

'Thank you, Poppy,' said Harry as he untied the blanket with his front teeth. 'I was saving the biggest apple for me, but you can have it. You deserve it!'

This time, Poppy was so glad Coco's friends were happy that she didn't feel shy or embarrassed. She just took a bite out of the juicy apple and kept on crunching until it was all gone. When she'd finished, she noticed that Coco had disappeared.

'Where's Coco?' she asked.

'I'm here!' purred Coco, scampering up to Poppy with a bunch of daisies. 'Lie down, Poppy, and shut your eyes – I'm going to give you a surprise.'

Poppy lay down with her legs folded underneath her. She closed her eyes. She could feel Coco playing with her mane – it was lovely. Her whole body felt relaxed.

Finally, Coco tapped Poppy on the nose. 'OK – ready!'

When Poppy opened her eyes she saw that Coco had woven a daisy chain into her mane. The little flowers looked like yellow and white jewels.

'Thank you!' she whinnied.

'It's so pretty!'

'Thank *you*,' replied Coco.

'You saved us from getting soaking wet. That rain is heavy – listen.'

Poppy pricked her ears. *Pit-a-pat, pit-a-pat* went the raindrops as they sploshed on the leaves of the oak tree.

Suddenly there was a loud *CRACK!* from high up in the sky.

'Uh-oh!' Bobbi cried. 'A thunderstorm!'

'Help!' squealed Harry. He covered his ears with his paws.

'I'm scared,' whispered Max, as another *CRACK!* echoed through the sky.

'It's all right,' said Poppy.

95

'Hide under my mane, you two little ones. You'll be safe there.'

'Wh-wh-what about the f-f-f-food?' Harry stammered as he and Max snuggled under Poppy's mane. 'What if it gets struck by lightning?'

'It won't,' Poppy said calmly as she gathered the remains of the picnic towards her with her tail. Coco and Bobbi cuddled up next to her tummy. Poppy felt very

brave and strong as she swooshed
her tail round to hug them close.

BOOM! went the thunder.
Poppy could feel Max and Harry
trembling. Coco and Bobbi were
shivering too. What could she
do to make them forget about
the thunder? Then she had an
idea. She'd have to be very brave
indeed, but maybe it would
work . . .

Poppy took a deep breath.

'Shall I tell you a story?' she asked. She gave a small sigh of relief. Her voice was still working!

'Yes, please!' said Bobbi.

Poppy cleared her throat.

'Once upon a time,' she began in a strong, clear voice, 'there was a baby Petal Pony called Pearl. Her legs were so wobbly she couldn't stand up.'

'Why were they wobbly?' asked Max.

'Because she was only one hour old, and she hadn't learned how to walk yet,' said Poppy. 'It's quite hard to get the hang of walking when your legs are as long as a Petal Pony's.'

'I'd be very scared if that was me,' Harry said.

'Pearl wasn't *too* scared, because her mum was with her,' Poppy said, 'and her mum was very nice and kind. "Come on, Pearl – you can do it," her mum said. So Pearl put her front hoofs on the ground and pushed until she was halfway up, and . . .'

BOOM! went the thunder.

All the animals cowered back against Poppy.

'What happened next?' Coco asked in a shaky voice.

'Pearl pushed and pushed with her hoofs, but her legs were still too wobbly. Bump – down she fell again,' said Poppy.

'Poor little Pearl,' said Bobbi. 'I hope there's a happy ending for her.'

'So do I!' said a gruff voice,

101

and a Bark Badger pushed his stripy face through the bushes.

Then a graceful Dream Deer stepped out from behind the tree. 'I'm sure there is,' she said, in a soft, soothing voice. 'But we'll have to hear the rest of the story to find out . . .'

Now there were rustling noises from all around. Lots of fairy animals were coming under the oak tree to shelter from the rain.

There were Stardust Squirrels and Hedgerow Hedgehogs, Bud Bunnies and Pollen Puppies – and they were all looking at Poppy and waiting for her to carry on with her story.

There was so many of them that Poppy began to feel a little shy again. What would she do if her voice stopped working and she couldn't tell the rest of the story?

POPPY THE PONY

She spotted a patch of pansies growing from the roots of the oak tree. She swished her tail softly over the purple flowers and a soothing perfume drifted out.

'Mmm!' sighed Max as he climbed out from under Poppy's mane. 'That smells nice. I'm not a bit frightened of the thunder now.' All the fairy animals who had gathered round were looking calm and happy too.

Poppy went on. 'Pearl's mum said: "Come on, Pearl, you can do it," and she nudged Pearl with her nose. "I can't!" said Pearl. "My legs won't work!" "They will," said Pearl's mum. "You've just got to believe it."'

Poppy paused for a moment. She looked round at all the animals. Their eyes shone as they waited to hear what happened next to baby Pearl.

They'd forgotten all about the thunderstorm.

'Pearl stretched out her front legs,' Poppy continued. '"I *can* stand up!" she said, and she pushed and she pushed until she was almost up, but then her legs started wobbling again . . .'

A whisper went up from the animals: '*Come on, baby Pearl! You can do it!*'

'Pearl's mum reached out with

her nose and she pushed against Pearl's tail so she didn't fall over again – and suddenly, Pearl was standing up!'

'Hooray!' cried the animals.

'Baby Pearl took one wobbly step, and then she took another. Then Pearl's mum trotted away!'

'No!' squeaked Max. 'What did Pearl do?'

Poppy smiled at him and carried on with the story. '"Don't

go without me!" Pearl whinnied. And suddenly she found that her legs were working! Faster and faster they went – until she was galloping after her mum! "I *can* do it!" Pearl neighed as she cantered along at her mum's side. "Yes, you can," her mum said. "And one day, you'll be the fastest Petal Pony in Misty Wood." The end!' said Poppy.

'Yay!' A big cheer went up

from all the animals.

They liked her story! Poppy
tossed her head, and flicked
her long mane with its pretty
daisy chain.

And the strangest thing
was that although everyone was
looking at her, Poppy didn't feel
the slightest bit shy.

CHAPTER SIX

Surprise!

Max fluttered his tiny wings and flew up beside Poppy's head. 'Was that story really about you?' he whispered in her ear.

'Yes,' Poppy whispered back. 'My mum helped me to stand up

when I was a baby. And one day, maybe I'll be the fastest pony in Misty Wood!'

'I bet you will,' said Max.

'The rain's stopped,' said Coco, looking up at the top of the oak tree. 'The storm's over!' The little Cobweb Kitten fluttered her wings and flew back and forth over the ferns. 'My wing's healed!' she called. 'Your story made me feel better, Poppy!'

Poppy swished her tail and neighed happily. Lots of other animals started coming over to talk to her. Poppy jumped to her feet, but there was nothing to be shy about. Everyone just wanted to be friendly.

'Your mane would make a great bark pattern,' said one of the Bark Badgers. 'Come and pose for us some time. Maybe you could tell us another story – and make everything smell lovely and sweet again?'

'Come round and visit us for snacks!' said a Stardust Squirrel. 'We've got some tasty hazelnuts!'

'Hazelnuts? Who said hazelnuts?' Harry cried.

'*Woof! Woof!*' barked a Pollen Puppy. 'How about a game of chase? Whenever you like, we'll be ready! *Woof!*'

A Dream Deer blinked shyly

at Poppy. 'Would you like to come running through the wood with us?' she murmured. 'You could spread the flower smells and tell us a story while we go!'

Max's whiskers were twitching again. 'I was just thinking,' he squeaked. 'You might be tired after all that running about and storytelling. Drop by my burrow and we'll make you a big comfy moss cushion to lie on.'

'I would love that! Thank you,' said Poppy.

Golden shafts of sunlight were shimmering through the branches now. The leaves and ferns of Misty Wood looked so fresh and green. All that was missing was the sweet smell of flowers. The rain had washed it away! It was time for Poppy to get going.

'I'll come and visit you all,' Poppy said to her new friends.

'And we'll have loads of fun. But first I've got my special job to do. Goodbye for now – and see you soon!'

As the fairy animals called their goodbyes, Poppy twirled her blue wings and floated away through the trees. The leafy branches were covered in dazzling raindrops that glinted in the sunlight, and a rainbow twinkled softly in the sky.

SURPRISE!

Poppy glided down and swished her tail over the bluebells and buttercups, roses and lilies, until Misty Wood was filled with the sweetest smells once again. Finally, as the sky was turning pink and the sun began to fade, she galloped back to Sundown Hill.

Her mum was waiting for her, looking worried. 'There you are, Poppy!' she neighed. 'Did you get caught in the rain?'

Poppy blew on her mum's nose to say hello. 'I was fine,' she said. 'The thunder was very loud though.'

'It was,' Poppy's mum said with a shiver. 'I was worried about you, all on your own in the storm.'

Poppy was about to explain what had happened when there was a flicker of wings close by. It was Max!

'Hello, Poppy,' he squeaked

as he fluttered past. 'Don't forget
to come and get your pony-sized
moss cushion!'

Poppy's mum's eyes opened
wide with surprise, but before
she could say anything, a Bark
Badger came trundling through
the grass.

'See you soon!' he called to
Poppy. 'Drop by any time!'

'Poppy! What's going on?'
asked her mum.

122

Poppy was just about to answer when a Dream Deer strolled past.

'Can't wait to go running with you!' the deer called softly.

Then a Pollen Puppy bounced up. 'See you soon for our game of chase,' he yelped, and then scampered away.

'Well!' Poppy's mum said with a smile. 'You *have* been busy, Poppy. Very busy indeed!'

123

She nuzzled Poppy's neck. 'And
what's this lovely daisy chain
doing in your mane?'

Poppy felt her heart swell
as she thought of all the fairy
animals she had met that day. Her

first ever friends! There was no need to be shy after all.

'A *friend* made it for me!' Poppy told her mum, who looked as pleased as Poppy felt.

Then Poppy kicked up her heels, neighed with joy, and cantered off to find a tasty patch of grass for her tea.

Turn the page for
lots of fun
Misty Wood
activities!

Picnic Time!

In the story, Poppy's new friends have a delicious picnic with lots of lovely treats for everyone.

What are your favourite things to eat at a picnic? Write them down here, and then draw them all on the picnic blanket on the next page.

1. ....

2. ....

3. ....

4. ....

5. ....

6. ....

Join the dots

Follow the numbers and join up all the dots to make a lovely picture from the story.

Start with dot number 1. When you've joined all the dots, try drawing Poppy's new friends all around her!

Fairy Animals

of Misty Wood

Meet all the fairy animal friends!

Look out for more Fairy Animals, coming soon . . .

Meet the

Fairy Animals
of Misty Wood

There's a whole world to explore!

Download the FREE "Fairy Animals" app and visit **fairyanimals.com** for lots of gorgeous goodies . . .

- Free stuff
- Games
- Write to your favourite characters
- Step inside Misty Wood
- Send us your cute pet pictures
- Make your own fairy wings!